Conversations with my dogs.

When my dogs converse with me
They do so in a Yorkshire accent.
They have managed to master the
Flat Yorkshire vowel sounds and the
Glottal stop syntax
That makes the accent so beautiful.

This is strange as one of them is a Schitzu,
Of Japanese origin,
The other a Bichon Frise
Of French descent.

They do occasionally throw in a word
I do not recognise.
I think these are swear words in their native dialect.

My dogs are jealous of my
Opposable thumbs.
They sit staring with envy as I
Open their food sachets and the
Tupperware treats box.

But when we go for a walk
They strut with pride,
Heads held high,
Tails curled over their backs.

"Look at me," they say.
"We are Dog".

(I am human," I say.
"We won't hold that against you, yooman," they reply).

Conversations with my dogs 2

We have just returned from a walk,
Probably a couple of miles.
Sniffed lampposts, dogs' bums, random bits of wall (my dogs, not me)
And had a run in the field.

I put the kettle on for a cup of tea.
Domino, my Schitzu, grumbles at me.
"What?" I ask him.
"Treat," he says.
"For what?" I ask.
"For walking with you." He gives me the 'why am I having to explain this?" look.
"So...you walked with me...and?"
"And you're having a cup of tea. We want a treat..."

He gets a treat.

I have just finished my tea.
Dexter, my Bichon, comes and nudges my thigh with his head.
"Non verbal communication," he smiles at me.
"It's time for a walk?" I smile back
"Got it in one," he grins.
"And you'll be wanting a treat when we get back?"
"Well done, yooman," he nods.

I, apparently, am learning.

Ten o'clock in the evening.
Domino comes and sits in front of me.

Just sits.
I look at him.
"Is this non verbal communication?" I ask.

"No," he mumbles.
"I'm just waiting."
"What for?"
"It's training time…" He doesn't add "stupid".

I get up, cut the cheese and he goes through his routine…
Sitting
Lying down
Rolling over
Standing on his two back legs.

It's then that I wonder…
Who is training who?

Conversations with my dogs 3

Sunday morning
Seven thirty
I was hoping for a lie in.
But…
They are shouting.
"Dad," they shout.
Over and over.
I have no choice but
To get up.

"What do you want?" I ask.
"A meeting," they say.
They look serious.
"A meeting?"
"Yes."
They strut into the kitchen.
I follow and make a cup of tea.
"Treat?" I suggest.
"Later. We need to talk."

This sounds serious.
"So," I pause.
"So," they echo.

"A meeting…"
"A meeting, yes," they agree.

Domino, my Schitzu, is sat in front of Dexter, my Bichon. He is the spokesman…

"We have lived with you for six years now…" he begins.

"And we think it's time for your appraisal," adds Dexter.

"Appraisal?"
"You know, to let you know how well you are doing as our yooman."

I can't believe they are going to pass judgement on my dog ownership…

"What if I don't come up to scratch?" I grin inside at the pun.
"Then we might have to look for another yooman…" Domino leaves the thought there.

Dexter clears his throat, but it's Domino who speaks.
"So, yooman. Strengths and weaknesses…"
Dexter is smiling.
I realise his throat clearing was really him trying not to laugh.

"Ah, yooman!" Dexter laughs.
"Gotcha!"
"Now get us a treat and get dressed…we need a wee!"

Conversations with my dogs 4

I hear them shouting as I get out of my car…
They jump up at me, licking my face, asking
"Where have you been?"
I have only been out an hour, to the supermarket.
"To the supermarket," I tell them.
They are not impressed.

"And what have you been doing, while I've been gone?"
"Waiting for you," replies Domino.
"Yeah, sitting on the stairs, waiting for you," agrees Dexter.

In the kitchen there is a box of tissues
Ripped to shreds
All over the floor.

"Boys…" I call.
They come padding in.
"Who's responsible for this?" I ask.
They both look away.
"You were the only two in the house…"
I leave the thought there for them…

"Burglars…" says Domino.
"Yeah, burglars," agrees Dexter.
"But there are no doors open, no windows broken…"
"Well, we shouted at them to go away…"Domino says, slowly.
He is thinking on his feet.
"But they wouldn't."
"Go on, " I say.
"And they were looking through the window…"

"Go on…"
"So we tore up the tissues to show how fierce we are…"
"Yeah, we're not to be messed with…" adds Dexter.

I smile.
"Now." I pause, look at them both.
"What really happened?"
Dexter clears his throat.
"We didn't know where you'd gone…"
"And we didn't want to starve to death…" continued Domino.
"So we tried eating those…"
"They don't taste good," moaned Dexter.

" I quite liked them," says Domino.

Conversations with my dogs 5

We are putting dog leads on,
Ready for our walk.
Domino looks at me and says
"What's it say on your tee shirt?"
"Born to Rock…"
I tell him.
There is also picture of an electric guitar
And an amp.
"Mmmm," he says.
"Why?"
"Because I like music…" I tell him.

"If I had a tee shirt," he says,
"It would say
"Born to run in fields with lots of grass and dog smells and birds,
And interesting things to wee on…"

"Too many words," I tell him.
"How many can I have?"
"Three…"

He thinks…
"Born to walk," he says.
"And the picture?"
"A big field," he smiles.

Dexter has been listening.
"What about you?" I ask.

"Easy," he says.
"Born to poo…"

I don't ask him what picture he would have

Conversations with my dogs 6

"Dad!" moans Domino, almost under his breath...
"What?" I ask...
"Are you not going to leave me with any dignity?"
I am washing his bottom, he is not happy...
"I have to wash you," I say. "You can't walk around with a dirty bottom..."
"I know," he says, "but leave me with some dignity..."
"How?" I ask.
"Close your eyes..." he suggests...
"Can't be done," I say.
"Well, can't you wear gloves or something?"
"I'm washing your bum, not doing open heart surgery..." I comment.
"Open heart surgery would be less undignified," he says...
"At least I'd be under anaesthetic..."
"It can be arranged," I mutter under my breath.

Dexter dances around us as I dry Domino...
"Your bum's wet," he laughs.
"See..." moans Domino..."no dignity and worse..."
He turns his back on me...
"No integrity left, either."

He dashes off to dry himself...
"Don't think I'm talking to you until I've restored some street cried..."
He mumbles to himself.

Conversations with my dogs 7

I am having tea at the kitchen table.
Domino plods up and sniffs...
"Sausages," he says.
"Yes," I agree. "Sausages."
"Can I have..."
He sits, waiting expectantly.
"No," I say.
"This is my dinner."
He cocks his head to one side.
"Your tea is in your bowl."

He strolls over to smell his bowl.
He looks back at me.
"Beef and carrots and pasta..." I tell him.
He sniffs it.
"Not sausages," he says.
"And it's out of a tin."
"It's your tea," I tell him.
"Sausages," he says.

I ignore him.

"I am sitting beautifully," he says.
"I deserve a sausage."

I ignore him.

"Look," he says. " Now I am sitting beautifully with my front paw raised."

I ignore him.

"Look now," he says.
"I am laid on my back showing my tummy. You are the pack leader.

You must feed me sausages."

I ignore him.

He lays on his front, head on his paws.
"You do not love me," he moans.
"I know this because you don't give me a sausage."

I let him sulk.

I finish my meal.
I have left one sausage.
"Would you like…"
Before I have finished my sentence he is up, licking my leg.

"Mmmm," he whispers. "Sausages."

He eats a piece I have cut for him.
Dexter trundles up behind him.
He gets a piece of sausage as well.

I look at Dexter.
"What?" He asks.

I look at him again.

"Okay," says Dexter.
"He does all the hard work and gets a sausage.
I wait quietly in my bed and get a sausage.
You work it out."

Conversations with my dogs 8

"Look at me!" shouts Dexter, when I collect him from the groomers.
He has a light blue bandanna fastened to his collar.
"I look like a gangsta dog!"
He struts around, grinning at me.
"Yooman," he growls…
"Gemme a treat, innit!" he says.

I look at him and try not to laugh.

Domino has a bandanna with skulls and crossbones decorating it.
He limps with one of his front legs.
"Look at me," he drawls…
"I'm a pirate. I just need a patch over my eye…"
"You need a parrot on your shoulder," I suggested.

He looks at me, thinking…

"Don't be stupid," he says.
"It would eat the treats."

Conversations with my dogs 9

"I need a wee…" Domino scratches at the kitchen door.
I open it for him, "Don't be long," I say, "It's late."

Dexter watches through the window…
"Do I need a wee?" He looks at me.
I shrug my shoulders, "do you?"
He thinks…
"Maybe…"
"Well, out you go, just in case…"

"I don't want one," Dexter shouts, from the bottom of the garden,
"But Domino's doing a poo…"
Domino ignores him, but comes back in and looks at me…
"Some things are private," he grumbles.
"But I'll be picking it up," I tell him.

"You must have a good collection by now," he says,
And smiles at me.

Conversations with my dogs 10

"Dad!" moans Domino, almost under his breath…
"What?" I ask…
"Are you not going to leave me with any dignity?"
I am washing his bottom, he is not happy…
"I have to wash you," I say. "You can't walk around with a dirty bottom…"
"I know," he says, "but leave me with some dignity…"
"How?" I ask.
"Close your eyes…" he suggests…
"Can't be done," I say.
"Well, can't you wear gloves or something?"
"I'm washing your bum, not doing open heart surgery…" I comment.
"Open heart surgery would be less undignified," he says…
"At least I'd be under anaesthetic…"
"It can be arranged," I mutter under my breath.

Dexter dances around us as I dry Domino…
"Your bum's wet," he laughs.
"See…" moans Domino…"no dignity and worse…"
He turns his back on me…
"No integrity left, either."

He dashes off to dry himself…
"Don't think I'm talking to you until I've restored some street cried…"
He mumbles to himself.

Conversations with my dogs 11

I am trying to teach my dogs a new trick.
I have two different coloured beakers and place a piece of cheese under one of them.
The dogs have to tap the beaker they think the cheese is under.
They sit and watch whilst I explain the rules and what I expect them to do.
Dexter cocks his head at me…
"You want me to do what?" he asks.
"Just do it," says Domino. "I want the cheese…"

I put the cheese under one of the beakers.
"Look," I say.
I cover the cheese with one beaker.
I show it again.
"Look, here it is," I say.
I cover the cheese again.
"Where's the cheese?" I ask.
Domino looks at me like I'm stupid.
Dexter wanders off…"what do I have to do?" he asks.

"I saw where you put it…" Domino says.
"You haven't moved it…" he looks at me.
"It's in the same place…" he almost tuts in disgust at me.
I give him the cheese.

"You insult my intelligence," he says.
"I will not play your game."
"I don't understand…" whines Dexter.

"Just give us the cheese…" mumbles Domino.
"I will sit, lie down, roll over and play dead," he says.
"I will even dance for you…"
"But I will not tap a beaker when you've shown me where the cheese is."

He seems pretty final about this.

"One more try?" I suggest.
"Just give us the cheese," he grumbles.

"What do I have to do?" asks Dexter.
"Just eat the cheese," instructs Domino.

I give them the cheese.
And again, I realise who is in control here.

Conversations with my dogs 12

Friday evening and I have just returned home from work.
The dogs are unusually quiet...
When I open the door I see why...
One of their dog beds, the medium size one, that lives downstairs,
Has been moved.
Not a few feet to the left, or
A bit closer to the door, but
Halfway up the stairs.

"What's happened here, the," I ask.
They both turn away from me.
"Ignore him," I hear Domino mumble.

"You can't get up stairs now, can you?"
Upstairs is where their water and food is.
"Not really..." begins Dexter.
"Don't look at him..." mumbles Domino.
Dexter turns his back.

"Dexter..." I say...
"Who, me?" He asks.
"Yes," I say, "you."
"I'm not Dexter," he says, not looking at me.
"I just wandered in..."

"Dexter," I say, trying to sound stern.
"What?" He asks.

"Domino?" I ask.
"What's happened with the dog bed?"

"What dog bed?"
He looks every where but at me and the dog bed.
"The dog bed that's halfway up stairs..."

"Oh," he mumbles,
"That dog bed."

Dexter comes up to Domino's side and nudges him.
"Don't tell him…" he says…
"He'll stop our treats or something…"

"You either tell me," I say, quietly,
"Or…"
"Or what?" says Domino.
I point to the smoke alarm on the ceiling…
"That," I say, "is a cctv camera…"
"A what?" Asks Dexter.
"It films everything you do," I tell him.
They look at each other and
Hang their heads.
"Sorry…" begins Dexter.
Domino gives him the look, one eyebrow raised.
He is not convinced.

"Let me help you out a bit here," I suggest.
"Have you been watching the dog channel on You Tube
And decided to ski downstairs?"

Dexter looks at Domino.
"What's You Tube?" He asks.

Domino steps forward a pace…
"If you're filming everything on that…"
He jerks his head to the smoke detector…
"How come you don't know about the wee
Behind the settee?"

I stop myself looking shocked…
" I know about…" I say.
I didn't.

"Oh," mumbles Domino.
"Oh," echoes Dexter.
"Oh indeed," I say.

"Never mind," I say.
"Let's put the bed back and forget about it, eh?"
Dexter stands up straighter,
Domino cocks his head on one side trying to
Work out the catch.

I move the bed.
The dogs bound upstairs and
Sniff round the kitchen,
Like it's some long lost place.

I think I might invest in CCTV.

Conversations with my dogs 13

"I need a favour…"
I am lying on the settee,
Suffering with a touch of man flu…
Domino has come to check on me,
But takes the opportunity to have a chat.

"What's that then, buddy?" I ask.
"I need you to write to the papers,
And talk to the television people…"
"Why?"
"Well," he says, "I've been reading…"
"Oh, yes?" I say.
"And what have you been reading?"
"Doggypedia…" he says.
"It's like Wikipedia, but for dogs," he explains…
"Okay," I say.
"And it appears dogs are getting overlooked…"
"Overlooked?" I ask.
"In the history of the world…" he explains.
"Oh," I say.
He looks at me…
"Explain…" I say.

"Well," he begins…"Everybody knows that a dog went into space
And that Lassie rescued kids down wells…"he continues…
But Schrodinger's cat, well…" he shrugs his shoulders…
"What about it?" I ask.
"It was a dog…Schrodinger's dog…"
"Right," I say.
"A dog…"
"Yep."
"And you read this in Doggypedia?"
"Yep."

"Anything else?" I ask.
"Well," he says, "you know the old TV programme, Skippy, the Bush Kangaroo?"
"Don't tell me…" I say…
"Yep," he says, "Skippy the bush dog…"
"No way," I say…
"Yep. Changed it because it didn't fit the tune."
"That explains it," I smile.

"Anymore?" I ask.
"Paddington bear…" he says….
"A dog?" I ask.
"A dog…" he agrees…
"I mean…" he says, "who ever heard of a talking bear?"

Conversations with my dogs 14

I have decided that the dogs needed to go on a diet...
I haven't told them yet,
I thought I'd just sort of...spring it on them...

We return from our walk...
They trundle upstairs and wait...
For a treat...

"Look what I've got for you..." I enthuse...
Dexter almost wags his tail,
His tongue lolls out of the side of his mouth...
He is in pre-drool mode...

"Is it something different?" Domino asks nervously...
He hops from one foot to another...
"Is it New?" He asks...
"You know I don't like New..."

Dexter sits, expectantly...
"Treat..." he moans...
"Let's see them first..." says Domino...

I get the packets and open them...
"Look," I say...
"Beef," I show them...
"Chicken," I show them...
"Lamb," I show them...

"They're small..." says Domino...
"They're treats..." Says Dexter...
"They are," I say to Domino...

"They are," I say to Dexter…
They each take a beef one…
Dexter wanders off into the front room to eat his,
Or feed his toys, his babies…
Domino, well, he sits and thinks…
"They're good," he says…
"But small…"
I agree with him…

"Because they're small…" he continues….
"In fact, less than a third the size of our normal treats…"
I see where this is going…
"Would it be possible to have another?"
"Try a lamb one," I offer…
"Don't mind if I do," he says…

Dexter darts in from the front room…
Skids to a halt…
"Lamb…" he mumbles…
I offer him in one…
" I need three more…"
"For why?"
"For my babies…" he says.

"I need to try a chicken one now," says Domino.

Conversations with my dogs 15

It is seven o'clock in the morning,
We have just returned from our morning walk...
I offer a treat...
Dexter takes it, wanders off...
Domino sniffs it, turns his nose away...
"These are not right,"he says.
"What do you mean?" I ask.
"They're a bit.." he thinks for the word...
"Bland,"he decides.

"It's all we have," I say.
He looks at me,
No tail wag
No raised paw.

"Dexter likes them,"I say.
"Well," he says,
"He's easily pleased..."

There is a tense pause between us...
He looks at me...
"Do you know my heritage?"he asks.
"Tesco's just doesn't do it for me..."

I wait.

"So," he finally says...
"When are you going to Sainsbury's?"
"Tonight," I say.

"I'll wait, then," he says.

I gather my things to go to work
And unlock the door.

Domino watches me from
The top of the stairs.
"Don't forget," he says,
"Sainsbury's ".

I wonder who is really the pack leader here.

Conversations with my dogs 16

We have put the dogs on a diet
Of sorts.
They have been told…
"But we're not fat," says Domino.
"No," I agree, "you're not."
"So why a diet?" He asks.

I show him a treat,
A chicken dumbbell…
"Too many of these…" I say,
"And not enough of this…"
I show him a dog bowl.

He looks at me like I'm speaking in Welsh.
Dexter saunters in…
"I can smell chicken dumbbells…" he says.
"They're going to starve us," Domino tells him…
Dexter looks at me…
Raises an eyebrow…
"Not true," I say…
"You just need to eat food…"

I explain the new regime…
A good morning treat,
A teeth cleaning stick,
One more treat later n the day
And the usual training treats.

They are not happy.

Later…

We are out walking...
Domino is walking slow, hanging back...
Dexter, just happy to be walking with me,
Trots along beside me.
Domino stops, sniffs some grass...
Dexter lollops up to him,
To share the inspection...
"Walk slower..." I hear Domino whisper.

We walk a little further,
A little slower.
Domino stops, looks at me...
"I am so weak..." he moans
And looks at Dexter...
"Me too," Dexter echoes...
"I need a treat..."
"You need to eat your food," I tell him.
He gives me The Look.
We get home...
Domino expects a treat...
I show him the dog bowl with his tea in it.
He walks to the kitchen door
And waits, telling me he wants to go out.
I open it for him
And he looks at me out of the corner of his eye before
Going out.
He stands at the top of the garden,
Checks I am watching...
And howls.
"My yooman is stopping my treats!" He shouts.
Social media for dogs...
I hear at least two answering barks...
He trots back inside...

"There," he says,
"The world knows…"

While this is going on
Dexter has eaten two bowls of food…
"Look," he says…
"I'm a good boy…"
Domino stares at him,
Goes over to sniff the bowls and
Walks off.
"I'll think about it," he says,
As he settles on the stairs.

Conversations with my dogs 17

It is late.
Training has been done.
Time to settle down and chill…

But no,
Domino scratches at the door…
"I need to go out…" he says.
"Okay," I say, thinking he needs a wee.
"It's cool out there," he says.
"You need to sort the heating out…"
"Sorry…" I say.

I let him out,
Watch as he sniffs and explores
And investigates…

Dexter watches too, then
Shouts…
"Dom!" He shouts…
"Dom!"

"He's okay," I tell him...
"What if something gets him?" He asks.
"Like what?" I ask.
"Like a..." he thinks...
"Dragon," he decides.
"You don't know what a dragon is..." I say.
"A whale then," he suggests...
"They live in the sea," I tell him.
He looks at me...
"A cat?" He asks...
"A squirrel?" He suggests...
"A tree?"
I look at him...
"I'll stop," he says.
"Yes," I agree.

I open the door...
Domino glances at me...
"What?" He asks.
"Dexter's worried about you," I tell him
"Let him worry..." he says.
"He'll be in soon..." I tell Dexter.
"I'll wait here," Dexter says.
He sits and watches,
Quiet now.

Conversations with my dogs 18

We are at Oakwell Country Park,
There is long, sloping field here,
A favourite with dog walkers
And picnickers in the summer,
But it is only April and the car park is almost
Empty.

I have brought the dogs here to
Try and teach them how to fetch…
I let them off their leads and they
Gallop away.

I call them back and,
Reluctantly they return.
They sit when I ask them to,
And I explain…
"We are going to learn a new game," I say…
"A game?" Gasps Dexter…
"Why?" Asks Domino.

"Let me explain…"
I pull a tennis ball out of my pocket…
"I throw the ball," I explain,
"Then you go and fetch it and
Bring it back to me…"
"Cool," pants Dexter…
"Why?" Asks Domino.

"Watch…" I say…
I throw the ball, not too far. And shout,
In my Exciting Voice…
"Fetch!"

They sit and look
At me,
Then at the ball.

"Show us…" suggests Domino…
I go and get the ball and
Bring it back.
"Like that," I say.
"I see," says Domino.
"Okay…" says Dexter,
But they both look a bit dubious.

"Let's try again," I suggest…
I look at them,
They look at me…
"Ready…"
"Yep," agrees Dexter…
I throw the ball…
They do not move.

"Go on then," I encourage them…
They trot up to the ball and
Sniff it.

"Bring it back…" I call.
"Why?" Asks Domino.
"Because it's called Fetch," I answer.
"Why?" Asks Domino.
"So I can throw it again…"
"Why?"
He walks back to me…
"I don't think so," he says.
"But it's good exercise," I say.
"This is how we exercise…" he says…
"Dexter…" he shouts…
Domino sprints off…
Dexter waits a moment, then
Dashes after him.
I watch them run in circles,
First one in front, then the other,
And they tumble over each other…
Until Dexter realises how far away from me he is…
He turns and rushes back to me…
Domino follows, slower, panting,
But smiling.

"See…" he says…
And he is right…
They are dogs, being the dogs they are,
Doing what they want to do,
Being the best dogs they can be.

We walk back to the car,
Happy.

Conversations with my dogs 19

The dogs are not happy,
Even though we are out walking.
It is windy and wet and they have their jackets on.
They don't like their jackets.

There are some wheelie bins that
Have been
Blown into the road.
Dexter stops,
And stares at the wheelie bins.
"Come on," I coax him…
"Are you sure?" He asks.
"I'm sure," I tell him…
"It won't hurt you…" I add.
"It's a wheelie bin…"

He starts to walk, but reluctantly,
And gives the bin a wide berth.

"What else are you afraid of?" I ask him.
Domino, interjects…
"Nothing," he says
"I'm afraid of nothing…" he repeats.
"I am your protector…" he says,
"I can't be afraid."

"What about thunder?" I ask…
"Well…" he grumps…
"Sometimes…" he admits.

"Big dogs," says Dexter,
"And leaves, and birds, and leaves…"
He thinks a bit more…"
"Sharks…" he adds.

"I'll make sure no sharks get you whilst we are
Out walking…" I say.
"Okay?" I ask.
"Okay," he says…
"Thanks."
He looks relieved…
"One less thing to worry about," he adds.

Conversations with my Dogs 20

The farmer who owns the fields where
We walk
Has decided to let the grass grow.
It is in anticipation of
His cows moving in and
Eating it or collecting it for winter fodder.

Dexter loves it…
He rushes into the high grass and crouches down…
"Look at me…" he shouts,
"I'm a lion…".
"Wrong species." I say.
"What?" Asks Dexter.
"Lions are cats…" I say.
Dexter looks at me.

Domino leaps in,
Like a child jumping into a swimming pool…
He bounds like he is on springs…

Dexter spreads himself…
Legs out in front,
Back legs stretched behind…
"I'm a snake…" he shouts…
"Wrong species," I say.
He trots to my side…

Domino is still bounding,
Like Tigger in Winnie the Pooh…

"He's a rabbit…" says Dexter,
"Or a kangaroo…"

Domino stops.
"I'm a dog, jumping in long grass," he says.
But heads back to us.

"I'd rather be a lion," says Dexter,
"Or a snake, hiding and sneaking…"
"I'm a dog," says Domino,
"And proud of it…"
He looks at Dexter in that way.

Dexter looks at him,
I see him thinking…
"Yeah," he says…
"I think I would too…"
They trot along beside me…
"But it's fun pretending," says Dexter.
Domino says nothing, but I can see
The smile on his face.
He looks at me…

'I was a good rabbit, wasn't I?" He says.

Printed by Amazon Italia Logistica S.r.l.
Torrazza Piemonte (TO), Italy